ON A RIVERBOAT JOURNEY

In the spring of 1767, Jakuchu and I journeyed to Osaka in a boat. As the scenery moved by, Jakuchu made sketches and I composed short poems. We did not care to complete our impressions. We worked on the spur of the moment, improvising by sheer inspiration.

ON A RIVERBOAT

A Handscroll by Ito Jakuchu

JOURNEY

with Poems by Daiten

Introductory Essay and Translation of the Poems by
Hiroshi Onishi

GEORGE BRAZILLER, INC.
NEW YORK

The author graciously thanks Burt Winther for
his assistance with the preparation of this text.

Reproduced from the Handscroll at The Metropolitan Museum of Art.
The Harry G.C. Packard Collection of Asian Art, Gift of Harry G.C. Packard
and Purchase, Fletcher, Rogers, Harris Brisbane Dick and Louis V. Bell Funds,
Joseph Pulitzer Bequest and The Annenberg Fund, Inc. Gift, 1975.
(1975.268.70)

For information address the publisher:
GEORGE BRAZILLER, INC.
60 Madison Avenue
New York, New York 10010

Library of Congress Cataloging in Publication Number: 89-62484

Printed and bound by Dai Nippon Printing Co., Ltd., Japan

Designed by Michael Mendelsohn

First published in the United States of America in 1989

First Edition

ISBN: 0-8076-1229-4

CONTENTS

ON A RIVERBOAT JOURNEY

Embarkation

Late in March 1767, the painter Jakuchu and the poet Daiten made a riverboat journey from Kyoto to Osaka. The work of art reproduced in this book is the product of their trip. The two friends set out in the morning from Fushimi, a small town just south of Kyoto that was a common embarkation point for Osaka-bound boaters. Having traveled seventy miles along the river, they arrived in Osaka after nightfall and disembarked at the wharf near Temmabashi bridge. The purpose of their visit was to see friends who were members of a literary circle in Osaka.

Watching the delightful riverside scenery from their small passenger boat while floating downstream, Jakuchu and Daiten were moved to vie with one another to see which could capture his impressions more poetically, each working in his chosen medium. The landscape reproduced here was based on the poems and sketches that resulted from this boatside rivalry. Although our facsimile has the form of an accordion album, the original is actually a continuous handscroll without any folded seams. In a radical departure from conventional handscrolls, which were executed in ink and brush, this scroll was printed in the unusual technique of rubbing, casting the landscape in a black-white reversal, a negative image. To follow the procession of scenes in the order in which Jakuchu and Daiten encountered them as they floated downstream from Kyoto to Osaka, the viewer must first turn to the back of this album and proceed from right to left, according to the conventional structure of Japanese and Chinese handscrolls. Thus, the handscroll begins with a view of the wharf at Fushimi and moves right to left through a continuous series of

views of the west bank of the river until reaching the Temmabashi bridge where the journey ended.

The castles, temples, shrines, mountains and villages that appear during the course of the handscroll were all famous for their historical significance or natural beauty. Known as *meisho*, such sights gave boaters on the Yodogawa the sense of traveling through the *topoi* of myth, legend and history. The Yodogawa had been a river of great historical importance since ancient times; it served as the major artery linking Kyoto, the former capital city, with the Inland Sea as well as the Uji River, which led in turn to the great lake Biwa. By Jakuchu's time in the Edo Period, the city of Osaka, at the mouth of the Yodogawa, had become a flourishing center of commerce. This increased the traffic of cargo and passenger boats on the river as well as the number of tourists who enjoyed boating as a recreational activity. Jakuchu and Daiten took a keen interest in the rich historical significance and natural beauty of the Yodogawa river basin and also demonstrated their awareness of the new level of activity on the river in their own day.

Pushing off from Fushimi, we encounter first a scene of a small boat being towed upstream by three men walking along the shore. The effort they expend to return upstream to Kyoto underscores the ease with which our boaters set out downstream. The artists probably took a small boat similar to this. A long stand of much-admired pine trees, known as the Senryo Matsu, stretches behind them along the river's edge. Next we come to an exquisite ensemble of natural and historic landmarks; the small Yodo bridge, the juncture of the Kamo River with the Yodogawa, and the tiered tower of Yodo Castle are clustered together in one picturesque scene. This castle, built by Toyotomi Hideyoshi, was a key monument of the Sengoku Period, the turbulent years immediately preceding the long peace of the Edo Period. The next landmark is an ancient shrine called Iwashimizu Hachimangu. Jakuchu created interest in this passage by counterpoising the *torii* gate of a second shrine, Rikyu Hachimangu, on the side of a mountain across the river from Iwashimizu. A single large crane, a symbol of divinity, flies suggestively near the *torii*. Soon thereafter, we arrive at Takahama, a retreat frequented by court nobles escaping the capital during the Heian Period. We then pass Maejima, Otsuka and Mishima, three rest stops where travelers took lodgings and meals.

After this, the boat passes Torikai, formerly the location of a pasture reserved for the emperor's horses. Moving next through a generous bend in the river, we come to Eguchi where, in previous centuries, men could enjoy themselves on moored boats serving as prostitutes' establishments. It was here that the noted twelfth-century poet Saigyo exchanged poems with a legendary courtesan, Eguchi-no-Kimi, who was immortalized with a tomb and shrine called Tatsudo, or Kimido, which became the object of a cult. An even fuller bend in the river takes us to Nagara, the site of a great bridge that had been the focus of several legends, though it no longer existed in Jakuchu's day. Approaching Osaka, we pass Genpachi-no-Watashi, the location of an important ferry crossing. Finally, we arrive at the pride of modern late-eighteenth-century Osaka, the great span of Temmabashi bridge. This image is portrayed with all the importance due to one of the most memorable sights along the river; its hovering arc looms overhead and designates the goal of the journey and the finale of the scroll.

The River Embraced as a Theme in Art and Literature

In 1672, a new shipping route was initiated to expedite commerce between the upper and lower parts of Honshu, the main island of Japan. As the southern terminus of this route, Osaka benefited tremendously from this commerce, becoming Japan's premier financial center in the eighteenth century. Since the Yodogawa was the main artery leading to Osaka, the growth of the city spurred an unprecedented surge in boat traffic on the river. The Yodogawa river basin became an increasingly active tourist area as well as a conduit of transportation. To facilitate this tourism, numerous guide books, maps and illustrations of *meisho* near the river were published. But it was the appearance of Yodogawa themes in novels, plays, paintings and prints that confirmed the new place of importance this river came to hold in Edo culture.

Perhaps the most striking image of the new popularization of the Yodogawa and its environs is a handscroll executed by Maruyama Okyo in 1765, just two years earlier than Jakuchu's handscroll. Okyo innovated a new form of riverscape painting based on cartographic methods curiously combined with minute rendering of sharply observed details; he painted the view of the east riverbank along the bottom edge of the handscroll and the west riverbank along the top edge. Since the river runs down the middle of the handscroll with the two riverbanks each facing the center, the handscroll has no up-down orientation, but is read from above like a map. Yet what the viewer sees is more like an aerial view of amazing detail than a map. So useful was Okyo's *ryogan zukan*, or depiction of both coasts of a river, to the popular explication of the river basin topography, that subsequent illustrators of tourists' guide books widely imitated his basic scheme in their illustrations of the Yodogawa river basin.

The new cultural importance of the Yodogawa in the Edo Period

was just as important an element in Jakuchu and Daiten's scroll as in that of Okyo. Moreover, since Okyo was a close friend of both Jakuchu and Daiten, there is little doubt that his Yodogawa handscroll served as a direct inspiration to them when they set about creating their own handscroll of the same subject just two years later.

Nevertheless, the two scrolls are more striking for their contrast than their similarity. Okyo maps out great masses of detail with minute precision, while Jakuchu abbreviates his imagery, focusing only on certain views that hold importance to him. Okyo demonstrates a great curiosity for all manner of objects and details indicative of contemporary life, while Jakuchu and Daiten introduce a more lyrical and expressive mood to the landscape. Perhaps the most conspicuous difference between the works is that of color versus monochrome. Okyo's delicate but realistic color scheme gives his scroll a mundane sensibility, which sets it sharply apart from the visionary quality of Jakuchu's severe arrangement of black and white. This monochrome landscape is further removed from ordinary vision by the eerie negative image that results from Jakuchu's highly unusual application of the rubbing technique of printing.

Realist or Fantasist?

However, we cannot simply conclude on the basis of these two Yodogawa scrolls that Jakuchu was the fantasist and Okyo the realist. For if Jakuchu's visionary negative image allies him with imagination, his greater fidelity to his observations of the landscape brings him across to the other side of the fence. Indeed Jakuchu attempted to restrict his picture to an illustration of the Yodogawa as he actually experienced it sitting in the ferry boat. While his mountains are depicted plausibly from a familiar boatside viewpoint, Okyo flies magically in the sky over the river basin and unfolds a landscape burgeoning with such intricate detail that his Yodogawa becomes an oneiric spectacle.

The comparison of these two views of the Yodogawa is equally paradoxical when considered in terms of tradition versus innovation. The structure of Jakuchu's landscape follows the tradition of the riverscape handscroll, while Okyo invents the unusual *ryogan zukan* format. On the other hand, Jakuchu's use of the rubbing technique to produce a negative image was exceedingly unconventional. In any case, the break with custom by no means separated either of these artists from their social context. Okyo's innovation facilitated an appetite for the description of facts that corresponded to a popular Edo-Period curiosity about the everyday social environment. Likewise, Jakuchu's illustration of the *meisho*, or famous places, to which Yodogawa tourists were attracted, indicates that contemporary popular culture was just as influential on his art. Ultimately, what sets Jakuchu's Yodogawa scroll apart from that of Okyo is not its originality or its reflection of contemporary social trends, but its expression of a very introverted and personal character that would be inimical to Okyo.

The contrast between Okyo's Yodogawa and that of Jakuchu corresponds to dramatic differences in their individual responses to the new social and cultural developments of their day. Japan experienced tremendous societal changes in this period as the traditional feudal power of the daimyo, or war lords, gradually deteriorated owing to the rapid development of a monetary economy. Consequently their patronage, which had been funneled through an elite group of privileged merchants, weakened its earlier domination of artists and craftsmen. Therefore, the work of artists such as Jakuchu and Okyo catered less to the taste of the privileged class and became more oriented to the anonymous public. This shift in patronage had a far-reaching impact on the lives of artists.

Okyo had a versatile talent which rose to the applause of the new public audience with inventions such as the *ryogan zukan* described above and the *megane-e*, an instrument resembling a camera obscura by which the artist demonstrated his fascination for the peculiar effects of Western naturalism. Although Jakuchu's response to these new conditions was just as original as that of Okyo, it took a very different form; he turned away from the feudal regimentation of art in previous periods and embraced the ideal of an untrammeled lifestyle. Freed from the demands and taste of upper-class patrons, his art was created for his own pleasure, or as an expression of his deep feelings towards his personal relationships. Perhaps his aesthetic stance is expressed nowhere as succinctly as in the title which Jakuchu and Daiten selected for their Yodogawa handscroll. The phrase *"jokyoshu"* conveys the impression of riding in a boat purely for one's own pleasure.

Riverboating with Rapture

Although the title *"jokyoshu"* is quite difficult to translate, it is an extremely cogent expression of what is perhaps the essence of the handscroll. Indeed, this phrase can serve as a symbol of not only the handscroll, but also the boat journey from which it originated and, in a more general sense, the lifestyle of Jakuchu and Daiten. Well versed in a partly Japanized form of Chinese like most

Japanese literati, Jakuchu and Daiten, or perhaps Daiten alone, created this title by playing with several Chinese-import words.

Each syllable in the transliteration of the Japanese pronunciation of this Chinese amalgam—*"jo-kyo-shu"*—corresponds to a single character in the original expression. The first two of these characters—*"jo"* and *"kyo"*—mean, respectively, "to ride" and "interest." Together they comprise a Chinese word—*"jokyo"*—meaning "as fancy dictates," "led by sheer inspiration," or "without any practical motivation whatsoever." The final character of the title—*"shu"*—means "boat." Its place in this title after the character *"kyo"* invites the reader to coin a new word—*"kyoshu"*—which would mean "boat of interest" or "boat of rapture." Conflating these expressions together, we arrive at a phrase that we might render as "riding a boat of fancy."

Thus, several layers of meaning are embedded in this utterance. It evokes the untrammeled lifestyle, boating with rapture and the delight of improvisation. In his postscript on the scroll, Daiten leaves no doubt that the last of these values pertains quite literally to this work. He writes that it was based on the poems and sketches that he and Jakuchu *improvised (jokyo)* on the boat trip. The appreciation of improvisation and the other aesthetic values expressed in this title identify the lifestyle embraced by Jakuchu and Daiten with that of their literati precedents in the tradition of the Chinese artist-scholar.

The importance of the Chinese literati tradition as an influential paradigm for the aesthetic values of Jakuchu and Daiten is underscored by a specific allusion to a legendary account of a fourth-century Chinese poet named Wang Ziyou. This moving story had traditionally been held as the epitome of the ideal of "being led by sheer inspiration," or *"jokyo,"* the element of the handscroll title described above.

One snowy evening, Wang Ziyou was reading a classical Chinese poem that described an invitation by a hermit. This inspired a sudden desire in Wang Ziyou to visit a close friend, a poet named Zai Andao. Although it was evening and his friend lived very far away, Wang Ziyou took no heed of practical considerations and promptly set off in a small boat to travel downstream on the river that led to his friend's house. By morning, the river had carried him near Zai Andao's house, but by then he realized that he no longer felt the urge to see his friend. So true was Wang Ziyou to his heart's impulse and so pure was his ideal of friendship, that he felt it would be futile to see his friend lacking the proper spirit, and he turned around to make the trip back home without even greeting his friend.

Daiten often likened his trips from Kyoto to Osaka to that of his Chinese literary forebear, and the handscroll which immortalized his and Jakuchu's trip to Osaka also grows in significance through its resonance with the legendary trip of Wang Ziyou. As in the revered legend of the Chinese poet, Jakuchu and Daiten rode a boat downstream to see literati friends living far off. Moreover, the title *"Jokyoshu"* suggests that they made this boat trip without any particular preparation or responsibilities, but merely in obedience to their poetic nature.

Yearning for Osaka

It is the river that functions as a stimulus to the imagination in both the legend of Wang Ziyou and the handscroll of Jakuchu and Daiten. The very same water that wets one's fingers will flow on through the riverbed across great distances, merging with other bodies of water until it ultimately unites with the ocean. For one who appreciates this character of the river, it serves as a metaphor for the blissful union of the self with other, a metaphor for transcendence. The effortless act of flowing with the current on a boat coasting downstream past great stretches of land gratifies a passionate sense of yearning for transport.

The Yodogawa had stimulated the imagination of centuries of boaters before Jakuchu and Daiten. Since ancient times, it had been used by pilgrims who journeyed to sacred places by boat. They would visit shrines near the river, such as the famous Sumiyoshi Shrine, or the Iwashimizu Hachimangu Shrine, which Jakuchu depicted on the west bank of the Yodogawa in his handscroll. Or, disembarking from their boats, the pilgrims would continue their journey by foot and head for sacred places such as the Kumano Shrine. In the Heian Period, a very different kind of boater joined the pilgrims on the Yodogawa as court nobles sought diversion from the rigid life in Kyoto by taking leisurely boat trips. These would be arranged as elegant pastimes for aristocratic passengers who would sojourn at retreats such as Takahama, which also appears in Jakuchu's handscroll. In the Edo Period, Yodogawa boating took on an entirely different character as the previously mentioned growth of tourism created a surge of middle-class recreational boating. Furthermore, boat journeys by the new type of artist in the Edo Period such as Jakuchu and Daiten added a new chapter to the history of boating, for their understanding of riverboating as an aimless yet refined aesthetic enthusiasm was a unique phenomenon.

Common to all these phases in the long tradition of Yodogawa boating was the different psychological connotations associated

with boating upstream to Kyoto, or *nobori,* as opposed boating downstream to Osaka, or *kudari.* The former suggested the ambitious dream of success motivating a strenuous trip to Kyoto, the time-honored capital city, whereas the latter connoted a sense of liberation, release and pleasure.

In the Edo Period, the sense of liberation implied by a trip to Osaka was more than a matter of coasting downstream with the current. While Kyoto had become an anachronistic city locked into a backward glance at its past glories, the burgeoning economic growth of Osaka supported the development of a whole new cultural milieu. This thriving city had become the focus of exciting new urban amenities, theaters, and centers of recreation such as the gay quarters. It was crowded with people seeking material gain, cultural stimulation, night-life excitement and just plain novelty. The new city renounced the old-fashioned culture associated with Kyoto and developed a culture uniquely its own. Furthermore, Osaka saw the rise of scholars, poets and artists from among ordinary townsmen of low birth. Indeed the whole city seemed to belong to a newly assertive middle class consisting of townsmen of independent means. Their access to the general prosperity enabled them to develop new popular institutions such as the famous Kaitoku-do, an adult school open to all citizens, established by scholars who were themselves simple townsmen. Together with Edo, Osaka also became a new publishing center, eclipsing Kyoto's former domination of this field.

In the mid-eighteenth century, the world of Japanese letters was ruled by "three capitals," namely Edo, Kyoto and Osaka. Literary circles thrived in each of these cities, and stimulating exchanges between them cross-pollinated their achievements. Cultured individuals met at literary gatherings where they read poetry, appreciated paintings and works of calligraphy, ate and drank, and bought and sold works of art. Osaka's literary circles had emerged in the early eighteenth century under the tutelage of their counterparts in Kyoto. By the second half of the century, however, Osaka rivaled Edo for cultural leadership, while Kyoto fell behind. Daiten, who was not only a poet but also a Zen monk of high standing, was regarded as a cultural mentor by many intellectuals in Osaka where he had played a key role in the formation of literary circles.

Kimura Kenkado, who provided lodgings for his friends Jakuchu and Daiten during their stay in Osaka, was the catalyst of an important literary circle in Osaka. He was born to a wealthy *sake* manufacturing family, but delicate health had caused him to remove himself from the family business. The heterogeneous collection that he accumulated reveals the range of Kenkado's interests; he owned Chinese and Japanese books, maps, paintings, works of calligraphy, plant specimens, minerals, coins, antique utensils and rubbings. He was also skilled in the arts of painting, composing poetry, seal-carving and calligraphy. Furthermore, as a precocious student of disciplines such as natural history, herbalism, botany and mineralogy, Kenkado authored numerous books on a wide variety of subjects. The reputation of this remarkable polymath spread throughout Japan and his literary gatherings in Osaka attracted intellectuals from far afield.

Jakuchu and Daiten, Painter and Poet

Kenkado was representative of the new style of literati which emerged in Japan in the mid-eighteenth century. Well-educated sons of wealthy merchants, these independent-minded intellectuals typically withdrew from the responsibilities of their families' businesses and devoted themselves to cultural pursuits. At the dawn of modern society, the urban culture which arose in Osaka and Kyoto, far from the more rigid political center in Edo, produced numerous individuals of this type. Though well-brought-up in good families, they deviated from the mundane lifestyle of their fathers. Nor could they subscribe to the establishment morality of the samurai ethic. In short, they were social misfits. Though Osaka produced such literati most prolifically, they were also common in Kyoto. The literary circles here were distinguished by the important role played by Zen monks who were dissatisfied with the conventional life of the monastery. As previously mentioned, Daiten was himself a literatus of this sort. The literary circle to which he and Jakuchu belonged in Kyoto was centered around another Zen monk, Baisao, who had left monastic life to enjoy an untrammeled and eccentric existence as a tea seller.

Since Jakuchu was the eldest son of a properous wholesale grocer in Nishiki-koji, a famous commercial market center that continues to thrive in Kyoto to this day, he was expected to take responsibility for his family's business. But after persevering for fifteen years, he found himself unable to continue to bind himself to this life. Therefore, he left the business to his younger brother and devoted himself to painting. It is not known precisely how and when Jakuchu began painting, but he had already been frequenting Baisao's literary circle when he made his commitment to art. It was in this circle that Jakuchu met Daiten. Having left his temple in 1759, Daiten concerned himself with poetry and lived the life of a member of the literati until 1772 when he assumed the eminent position of abbot at Shokoku-ji, one of the most presti-

gious temples in Kyoto. During the intervening thirteen years, however, Daiten absented himself from temple life and kept the company of like-minded friends outside the Buddhist community.

Jakuchu looked up to Daiten as a mentor in Zen Buddhism as well as in art, and the latter reciprocated without any sense of pedantism. It was Daiten who selected the pseudonym "Jakuchu" by which his painter friend was to become known. "Jakuchu" means "like emptiness" and was borrowed from Laozi's phrase, "Fullness is like emptiness in its appearance." In this spirit, Daiten frequently counseled his friend to paint for his own sake rather than gratify others by puffing up his work with showiness.

Likewise, when the two friends set out on their riverboat trip in 1767, they were not traveling for extrinsic or *a priori* reasons but believed themselves to be acting for their own sake, led by sheer inspiration. As in the legendary boat trip of the Chinese poet Wang Ziyou, they were moved purely by the desire to see their friends who could be reached by floating downstream.

Details of their trip and subsequent sojourn in Osaka can be uncovered in the twelve volumes of the collected writings of Daiten, entitled *Shoun Seiko.* This work groups Daiten's prolific writings according to the various literary forms in which he wrote. Within these categories, essays and poems are chronologically arranged, so it is possible to locate passages written at about the time of the boat trip to Osaka. It is from this source that we learn that the two friends traveled on the Yodogawa in late March and that they stayed with Kimura Kenkado in Osaka.

On April 3, they took another riverboat trip, this time on the Nakatsu River of Osaka. On this trip they enjoyed music and composed poems in the company of another prominent poet, Katayama Hokkai, and some members of Konton-sha, his literary circle. Daiten and Jakuchu remained in Osaka throughout the summer and autumn. They occupied themselves by attending poetry readings and gatherings where paintings and works of calligraphy were appreciated and by making outings to shrines, temples and hot springs in the Osaka area. Passing from one diversion to another as fancy moved them, the two friends whiled away six months in Osaka with no thought of hurrying back to Kyoto. Indeed, though they had no idea of staying away so long when they left Kyoto in March, they did not return home until half a year later, in mid-September.

The initial riverboat journey that brought Jakuchu and Daiten to Osaka set the tone for this long, unplanned summer of aesthetic diversion. From morning to evening, the two friends had sat making sketches and composing poems in their boat moving downstream on the Yodogawa. Their handscroll preserves the sense of a boatside dialogue between artist and poet, each interpreting the scenery in his preferred art. The previously mentioned depiction, for instance, of two shrines on opposite sides of the river, suggests the nature of their collaboration; one imagines Jakuchu sketching this scene as Daiten notices that "A white crane flies high in the blue sky," and jots down this line on his page of impressions. This in turn prompts Jakuchu to catch a quick sketch of the bird before it disappears over the horizon. We cannot be sure who saw what features of the landscape first, but the completed handscroll preserves the spirit of a spontaneous interchange between friends stirring each other with their witty imaginations. For in the handscroll, flying in the sky above the two shrines next to Jakuchu's image of a bird, is Daiten's simple observation in his own calligraphy: "A white crane flies high in the blue sky."

In his postscript on the scroll, Daiten states that his own poems as well as Jakuchu's sketches were incomplete fragments improvised during their boat ride. The twenty-two poems that hover in the sky above the Yodogawa riverbank are incomplete indeed. Although these simple observations are written in the form of a four-line Chinese verse, Daiten chose to compose only two lines for each poem. The resulting "half-poems" read more like the fresh, direct thoughts expressed in Japanese *haiku* poems than Chinese verses, though Daiten did write them in Chinese.

Jakuchu and Daiten delighted in the jostling of their words and pictures in piquant contrasts. For example, at Genpachi-no-watashi, Jakuchu depicts a small temple in a grove of trees at the river's edge. But, Daiten interjects, "Deep in the forest, a temple is unseen. The evening bell is heard only at sundown." The artist, it seems, observes the temple, which the poet can only imagine, and turns a deaf ear to the bell, which tolls as an emblem of sunset for the poet. With the stimulation of this subtle friction between poem and picture, Jakuchu and Daiten must have enjoyed each other's company greatly and their boat trip must have seemed to pass quickly.

The Art of the Handscroll

We have characterized the imaginative disposition of the artists of this handscroll as improvisatory and spontaneous. It would be far from accurate, however, to consider the handscroll itself to be the product of improvisation alone. A great deal of aesthetic deliberation separates the assortment of improvised sketches and fragments of poems that Jakuchu and Daiten carried off the ferryboat and the landscape reproduced here. Enormous technical

effort and ingenious contrivance were required to organize and amalgamate the fragmentary sketches into the rhythmic flux and continuum of the long riverscape realized with great sophistication in this large-scale handscroll. To be sure, even in the completed state, which was achieved by the impress rubbed from a series of woodblocks, the contours of mountains, trees and houses retain the fleeting, spontaneous quality of sketches executed rapidly in a boat moving swiftly downstream. But the careful pacing of the river views in a fluctuating yet continuous flow could only have been achieved after the artist disembarked from the boat, when he put his mind to the task of composing a single unified handscroll landscape. Moreover, the decision to execute this work as a colorless rubbing in sharply contrastive black-and-white resulted in a reconstruction of the landscape in an entirely new mood, endowing this memory of riverboating with an unforgettable rhapsodic tone.

As previously mentioned, Jakuchu and Daiten were surely influenced by the recently completed Yodogawa handscroll by their friend Okyo when they set about forming their impressions of the river into a handscroll of their own. Nevertheless, they were also undoubtedly aware of the long tradition of riverscape handscrolls which preceded Okyo. This tradition can be traced back through the history of Chinese painting to as early as the fourth century, when Gu Kaizhi painted "Nymph of the Luo River." Subsequently, Chinese painters reformulated the riverscape to the requirements of mythical themes, such as river gods, as well as literary themes, such as the picturesque tour. Painters also depicted actual rivers in China in the handscroll format. Li Gonglin, for example, painted the River Shu, and Ma Yuan painted the Yangzi River several times. Perhaps the most common river subject in Chinese painting was "Eight Views of the Xiao and Xiang Rivers." Chinese rivers also appear in Japanese painting. Sesshu, for example, was said to have painted a scroll of the Yangzi River based on sketches made during his travels in China. Like the theme of the river, that of the journey also links Jakuchu's handscroll with important precedents in the Chinese and Japanese history of handscroll painting. In particular, Japanese painters of *emaki,* or narrative picture scrolls, frequently wove the theme of travel into the progressive structure of their imagery. Thus, the order of the succession of landscape scenes that appear as the viewer progresses through the *emaki* is justified as the representation of the path traveled by the heroes of the narrative.

That the journey and the river are frequent themes in the history of the handscroll is no accident, for the physical character of this painting format is remarkably congenial to the depiction of these subjects. The long, thin shape of a handscroll fosters the association with a river, and the time which passes as the viewer follows the imagery of a handscroll from right to left is analogous to the time which elapses during the course of a boat trip. Moreover, the fact that a handscroll has a beginning and an end, a feature that is quite unusual among painting formats, conforms to the structure of a journey. Even the capacity of a handscroll to be rolled up into a compact cylinder equates it metaphorically with travel, for the memory of spatiotemporal experience is preserved in a capsule. By placing their sketches and poems within the flux and continuum of a composition dictated by the handscroll format, Jakuchu and Daiten succeeded in opening the fleeting memory of their journey to unlimited rediscovery.

Black Sky and White Light

Although Jakuchu worked within the long tradition of the riverscape handscroll described above, there is virtually no known precedent for *printing* a landscape on a handscroll of such large scale as this. Furthermore, the printing method he used, rubbing, was an exceptional technique to use for pictures as it had hitherto been viewed almost exclusively as a means of printing texts.

This technique of rubbing, or *taku-hon*, originated in China, where it was used to transfer inscriptions or patterns incised on the surfaces of objects, such as *steles* and bronze vessels, onto paper as an act of commemoration. Wet paper would be pressed against the surface incised with the design to be transferred such that the paper would sink part way into the incisions of the relief. Then ink would be applied to the paper with a small pillow-like device filled with a soft material such as cotton. This would blacken the paper everywhere except where it was recessed in the lines of a design or inscription. Thus, the impression obtained by rubbing is necessarily a negative image of the prototype, and it is this black-white reversal that gives this technique its unique character.

The *taku-hon* method of printmaking came to be used for the production of books illustrated with samples of fine calligraphy to be copied by students. Here, too, the intent of the rubbing was not just to reproduce the model but to commemorate a masterpiece from history. The prototype deemed worthy of emulation would originally have been executed in brush and ink on paper. The brushed characters were then transferred onto a stone slab or wood block by carving an intaglio relief into the hard surface. The rubbing process was then carried out on the resulting slab or block.

The *taku-hon* method appeared in Japan sometime before the Edo Period, when scholars and antiquarians came to use it frequently. They employed this technique for the reproduction of texts for calligraphy model books and to copy the inscriptions and designs on many sorts of antique artifacts. They appreciated the classical appearance and enduring character that texts and designs would assume when printed in this manner. The printing of pictorial images by the *taku-hon* method, however, never became a widespread practice; other than this scroll and other works by Jakuchu, no such images are known to have originated in Japan, and those from China are exceptional.

Jakuchu must have executed a handscroll in black ink on white paper in the customary manner before the landscape was made into a print. This painted image was probably then given to a carver, possibly a certain Rai Keisen, known to have carved blocks for later rubbings by Jakuchu, who cut incisions into the surface of wood blocks following the black strokes of the brush. When these blocks were rubbed, the image underwent an amazing transformation as black and white were reversed. The shift from ink monochrome painting to negative-image print was achieved by a process of the greatest technical simplicity. Yet the character of the landscape was completely transmuted by the utterly unprecedented use of this primitive technique.

Though the artist abruptly broke with tradition, his scroll should not be thought of as a mere curiosity intended to entertain its audience by the oddity of its technique alone. Jakuchu was not content simply to display the rarity of his technical invention; he discovered the expressive potential unique to this novel medium and adapted it masterfully to his landscape subject matter. This artist, whose oeuvre is quite varied, characteristically worked with great sensitivity to the medium he selected. In 1766, just one year before producing the Yodogawa handscroll, Jakuchu completed a series of thirty hanging scrolls of animal and plant subjects. In these works, executed in colors on silk, Jakuchu used an unusually brilliant palette with daring combinations to produce striking effects. In the Yodogawa handscroll, too, Jakuchu demonstrates admirable command of his technique.

The primarily scriptive tradition of the *taku-hon* rubbing technique included two basic methods: *ukin-taku* and *senyoku-taku*. The former produced a thick, dark coat of ink, while the latter yielded a lighter image with softer contours. Jakuchu struck upon the ingenious idea of combining the two methods in a single work of art. He reserved *ukin-taku* for the sky, which is thereby covered with a thick, rich blanket of black ink. *Senyoku-taku* is responsible for the softer greys, which represent the land masses. The subtle tonal gradations were probably obtained by skillfully manipulating the ink with the cotton-filled swab, though some sort of blowing technique has also been proposed to explain the delicate granular effects achieved.

With this original application of unconventional techniques, Jakuchu created an image of unusual power. The thick, dark blackness of the negative shapes in his composition causes them to exert an intense pressure on the white shapes and contours. Since the latter shine with a piercing luminescence, they easily hold their own against the powerful blackness of the surrounding *ukin-taku*. This rivalry of black and white, positive and negative, electrifies the composition with an arresting sense of tension.

The conversion of a brushed black line to a carved incision and then to a white area surrounded by rubbed black ink represents a crystallization of the fluidity of the ephemeral brush path into a frozen sculptural condition. The retention of the spontaneity of the stroke in this more permanent form charges the imagery thus produced with a compelling kinetic potential. Thus suspended in a state of timelessness, the transitory experienced moment is memorialized.

The inky black sky hanging over the riverbanks brings a fantastic and extraordinary quality to this landscape. The large areas of the composition given to unmodulated black ink make the picture as flat as a blackboard. Yet a delicate sense of depth resonates within the implacable flatness of this surface. The paradoxical inseparability of this exquisite landscape space with the flat picture surface casts the scenery into an otherworldly silence, an exalted state of rapture.

Despite this capacity of the scroll to draw the viewer out of this world to an ethereal realm, this spectral landscape is carefully grounded in the sensory facts of the artists' riverboat journey. One feels the glare of the morning sunshine reflecting on the water surface in the opening stretches of the river by virtue of its contrast to the black sky above. Similarly, light glistens in the leaves of the trees surrounding Yodo Castle and Iwashimizu Hachimangu Shrine. One even senses, despite the unvarying blackness of the sky, a subtle passage from daylight to twilight. This is achieved two thirds of the way through the scroll at the hamlet of Eguchi, where the land mass, which had thus far been differentiated from the sky by its lighter grey tone, disappears into the blackness of the sky. Finally, as we approach the end of the handscroll, crepuscular light bathes the distant mountains hovering on the horizon in the setting sun.

These times of the day are knitted one to another and integrated within the whole landscape by means of the continuous pulse of the light-and-dark rhythm from the beginning to the end of the scroll. Changes are orchestrated within the structure of continuity. The flow of light oscillates within the dictates of a controlled rhythm. The horizon strikes at the black velvet, subsides and continues as before. The amplitude of the swollen convexity of the river where it bows outward at Nagara is prefaced by two congruent bends of more modest dimensions. This final turn of the river announces the approach of Osaka, the destination of the journey. In the evening glow of the final stretch of the handscroll, the landscape relaxes and closes over distant mountains with a sense of release.

Improvisation and Commemoration

The abruptness with which Jakuchu introduced the rubbing technique to the tradition of the riverscape handscroll raises questions concerning the relationship of Jakuchu's initial intention to his results. Did the striking effects we have described arise in accord with his expectations? Did he select the rubbing technique because he wanted to produce precisely those features we have attributed to it? Since this handscroll is the first known work by Jakuchu produced by rubbing, it is probable that the creative process was experimental to some degree. Moreover, immediately after this work, in 1767 and 1768, he deployed the *taku-hon* method again in two albums of bird and flower images accompanied by Daiten's poems. It is tempting to think that Jakuchu's impulse to adopt the *taku-hon* process to the handscroll format came to him by accident. Initially, at least, he may have engaged himself in the process of the rubbing method without any clear idea of the results it might produce. But he must have learned quickly from this first encounter and then felt the desire to exploit the potential of the medium more fully. Perhaps prior experimentation gave him the confidence to deploy the technique on a work of the complexity and large scale of the Yodogawa handscroll. In the albums that Jakuchu was to print after the scroll, he would use this new technique with even greater sensitivity, producing graphic images unthinkable in the traditional medium of black-ink painting.

However, the role of accident in Jakuchu's achievement must not be overstated. Although there were no prototypes for large-scale landscapes executed by the rubbing method, rubbings of calligraphy were popular among Edo-Period scholars and artists; Jakuchu's friends, Kimura Kenkado and Baisao, included them among the aesthetic objects in their collections. Though rare, rubbings of pictorial imagery were to be found in China. Moreover, the Edo Period produced a culture of rare sensitivity to the expressive potential of many sorts of printing. Modern industrialized mass printing has perhaps denuded this medium of the extraordinary expressive power it had in its more primitive forms. Living in a society which distributes information without dependence on woodblock printmaking, our responsiveness to this medium has deteriorated considerably. Jakuchu lived during a time when even printed matter of the most mundane sort had the rich texture of the woodblock impression. Ukiyo-e prints, a high point in the history of the printed image, served as popular broadsides. Polychrome woodblock printing had been invented by Suzuki Harunobu just two years before Jakuchu's scroll was printed. Artists were also developing the more refined and exquisite form of printing known as *surimono* at this time. Edo-Period literati watched these impressive new developments in printing with keen interest. Daiten, for example, expressed his amazement at the extraordinary technical advances in Ukiyo-e printmaking in a comment to a poem in his collected writings, *Shoun Seiko*.

Moreover, a general climate of innovation in the eighteenth century provided the supportive cultural context for Jakuchu's daring shift of a conventional subject out of its customary medium. Men such as Hiraga Genai absorbed themselves with the study of Western knowledge and new ideas. We have already considered the invention of the *ryogan zukan*, or illustrations of both coasts of a river, by Jakuchu's friend Maruyama Okyo. Thus, Jakuchu's originality was not an isolated phenomenon.

No doubt the desire of Jakuchu and Daiten to give several of their friends copies of the artistic product of their boat trip underlay their decision to produce their handscroll as a mutiple. As the lack of any publisher's mark indicates, Jakuchu's scroll was not published for public distribution in the manner of contemporary Ukiyo-e prints. The handscroll was not intended for the anonymous public but for an intimate group of individuals selected from among the members of the literary circles to which the artists belonged. Here we see the inevitable dilemma of the artist, whose creative activity is, in its essence, a very personal, intimate endeavor but who, nonetheless, wishes to communicate with at least some part of his social environment. How then did these artists arrive at the rubbing technique of printmaking as the vehicle for their project?

Perhaps Daiten's calligraphy offers the most direct reflection of the route by which the artists moved their riverscape out of the category of conventional ink monochrome painting and created

an unheard-of-anomaly, a *taku-hon* picture scroll. The reproduction of Daiten's poems by means of rubbing was entirely consistent with the traditional scriptive application of this method. His elegant calligraphic works of art were preserved and commemorated by carving them in wood and then transferring them to the paper scroll by the rubbing process.

It is the carrying of the landscape imagery into this medium along with the calligraphy that violated expectations and crystallized the traces of improvisation. The carving of Jakuchu's sketch-like brushwork in wood enabled its transference through rubbing to a small set of reproductions. This somewhat paradoxical melding of improvisation and commemoration posed a viable resolution to the contradictory aims of the personal creative act and the desire for communication. Thus, the results achieved by Jakuchu's transgression of the conventions of the riverscape handscroll were indeed promising, but it was to remain an innovation without subsequent elaboration by other artists.

In the two centuries that have passed since the boat journey of Jakuchu and Daiten, the Yodogawa has changed beyond recognition. Industrialization has brought golf courses and parking lots to the riverbanks. Where Jakuchu saw dormant villages, there are now concrete apartment towers erected to house suburban dwellers who commute to workplaces in Osaka. Only the profiles of the distant mountains still resemble Jakuchu's likeness. Today the crust of modernity creeps over more and more of the riverbanks, and the Yodogawa topography has lost all traces of the experience of Jakuchu and Daiten. The memory of their journey is retrievable only through their handscroll. In this sense, the handscroll is a historical record. Yet it was hardly a documentary project; the two friends discovered personal and subjective meaning in their environment and expressed these meanings in an introverted vision. The broader significance of their work of art lies in its contribution to one phase of the ongoing process of the enculturation of the landscape. Layer upon layer of meaning—mythological, religious, political, economic and socio-cultural—accrued to the Yodogawa river basin from the imagination of its inhabitants and those who passed through it during the course of centuries. Jakuchu and Daiten expressed their particularly intense experience of one moment in this history. This moment arose from the social climate that flourished along the Yodogawa in their day, a time when the river served as the crucial artery for a community with a rare balance of economic prosperity, ecological equilibrium and cultural innovation.

The Handscroll begins at the back of the volume

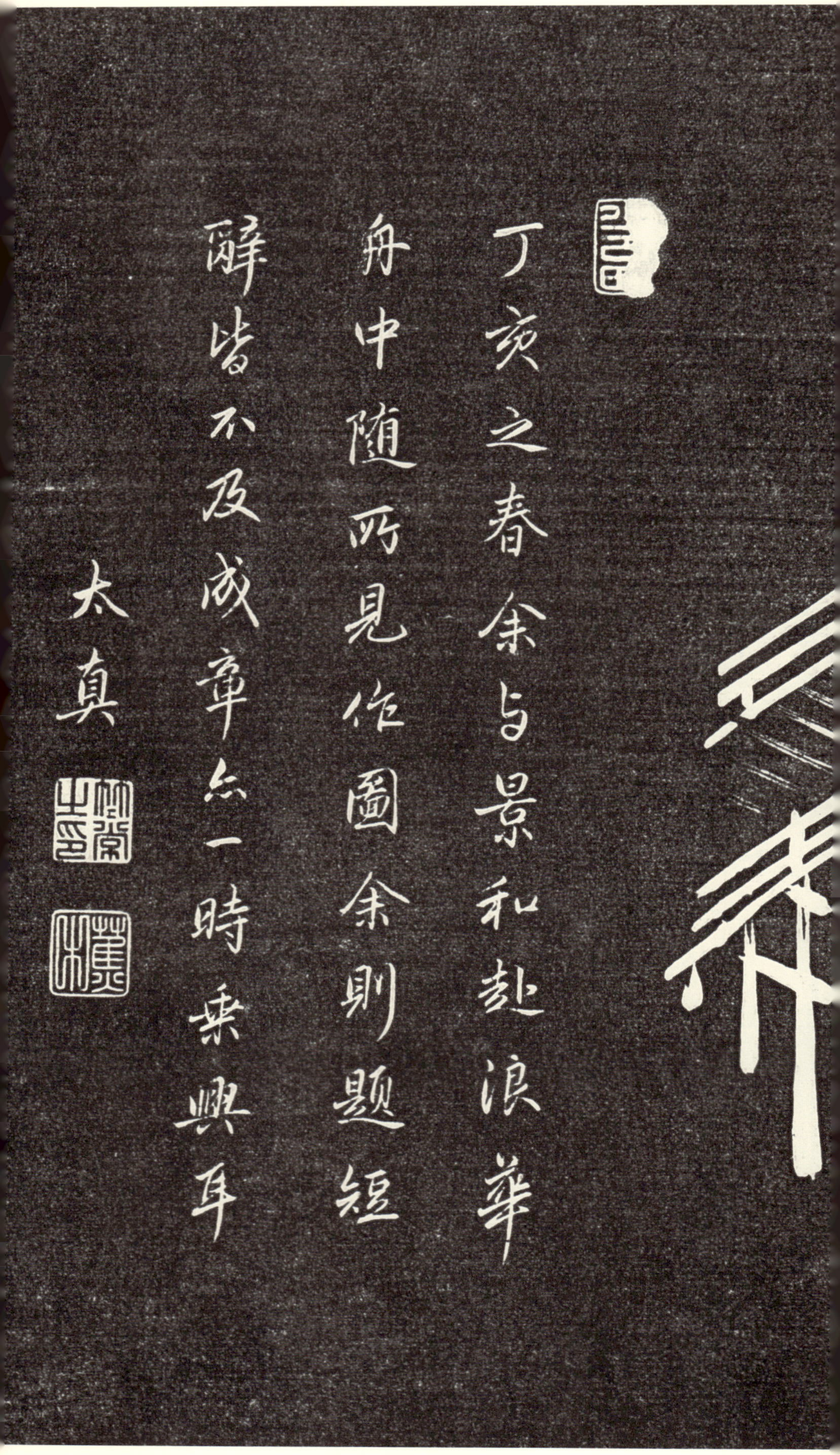

In the spring of 1767, Jakuchu and I journeyed to Osaka in a boat. As the scenery moved Jakuchu made sketches and I composed short poems. We did not care to complete our impressions. We worked on the spur of the moment, improvising by sheer inspiration.

Beneath the three-hundred-foot span of a great bridge,
Thousands of boats come in to moor.

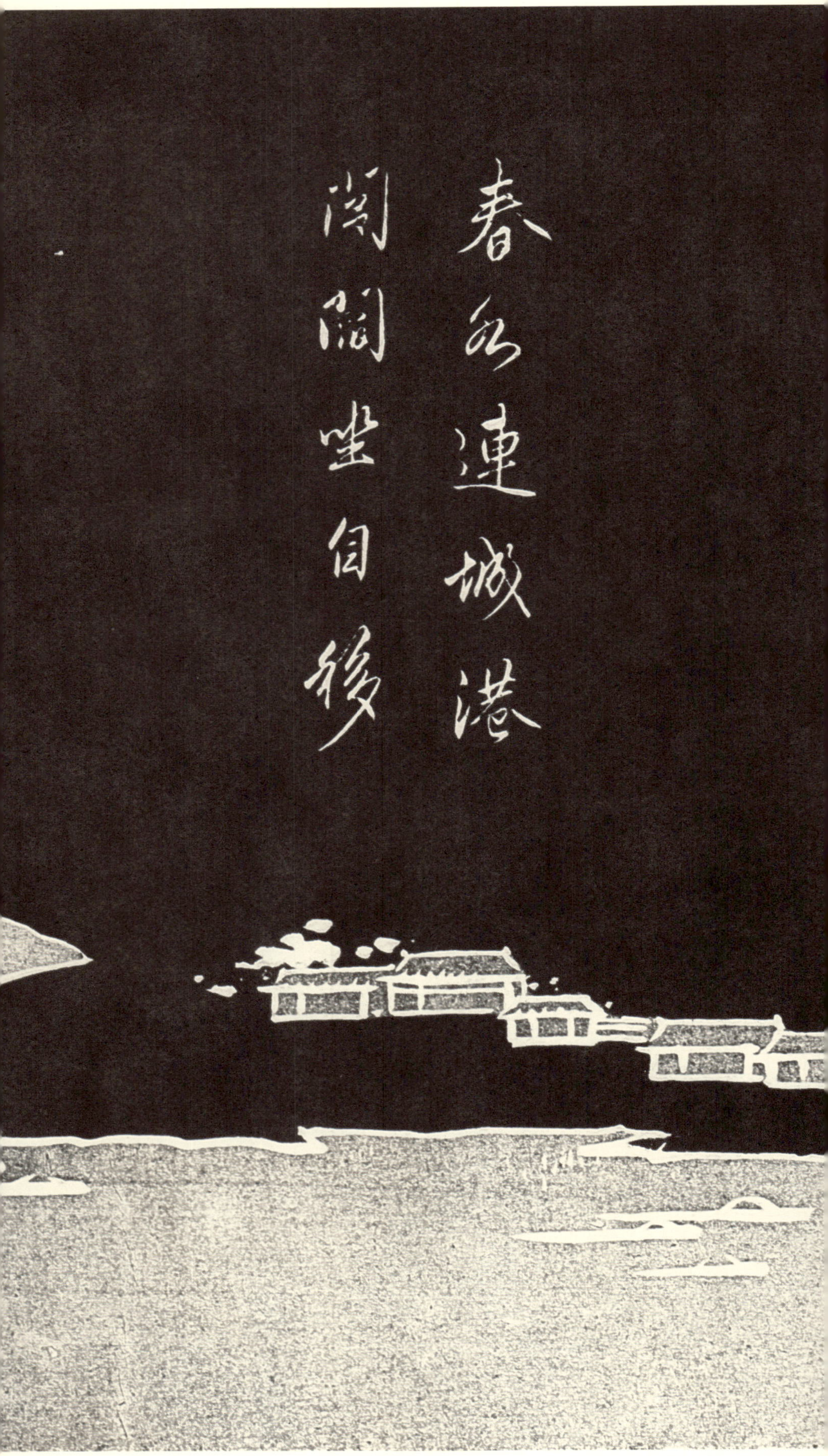

Spring water flows to the Osaka waterfront.
The changing cityscape passes while we sit in our boat.

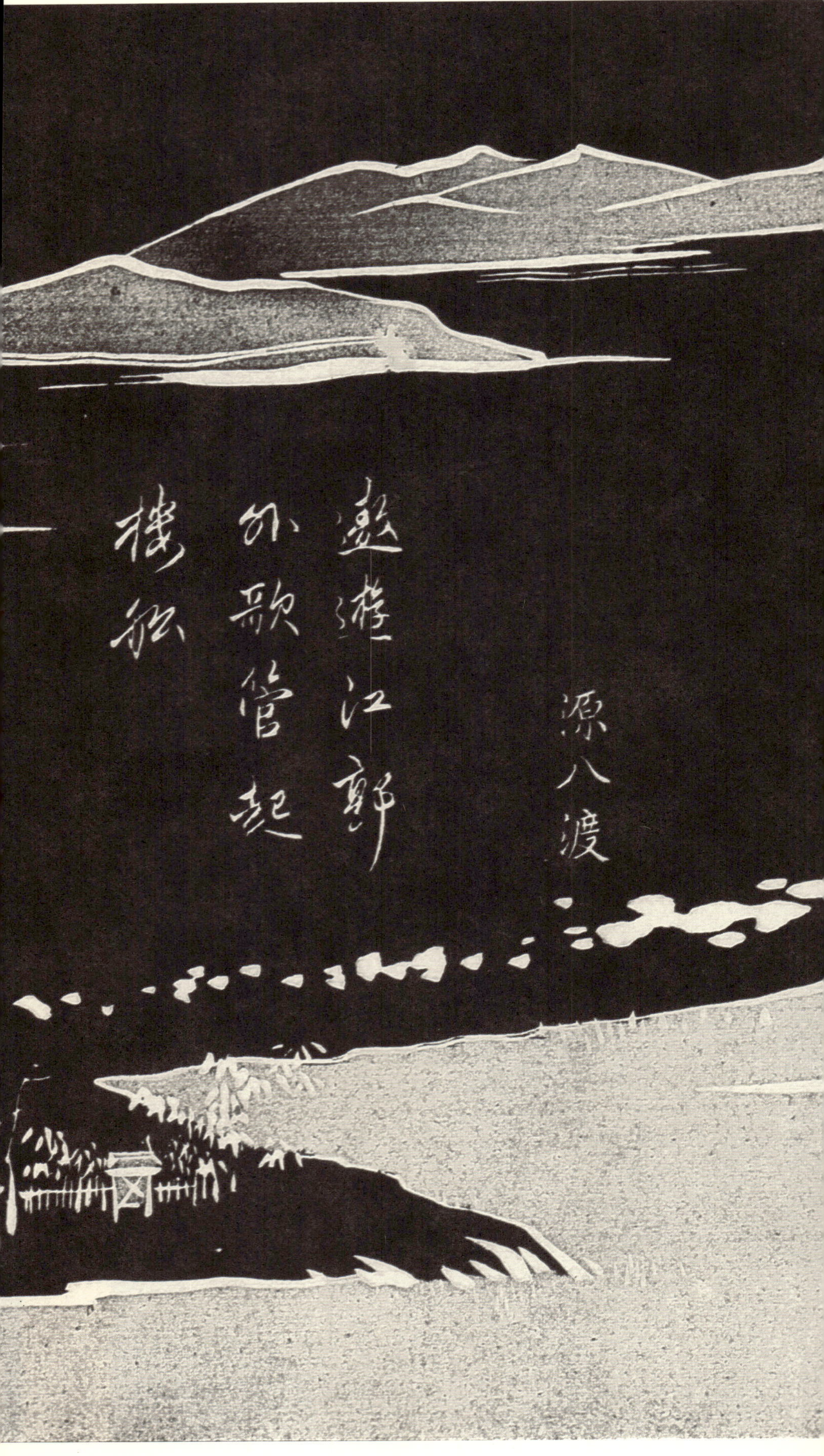

Place of entertainment by the water's edge.
Revelers sing to music in pleasure boats.

Deep in the forest, a temple is unseen.
The evening bell is heard only at sundown.

Waving their wings,
Ducks and herons swim and fly.

Kudzu cloth lies bleaching on the white sand.
Though spring winds blow, people are still afraid of snowfall.

長柄

The sun sinks in the sky and the west winds rise.
Do they sink and rise with one mind?

Oh traveler! From what distant place have you come?
I'll wait for you at a tavern.

達堂

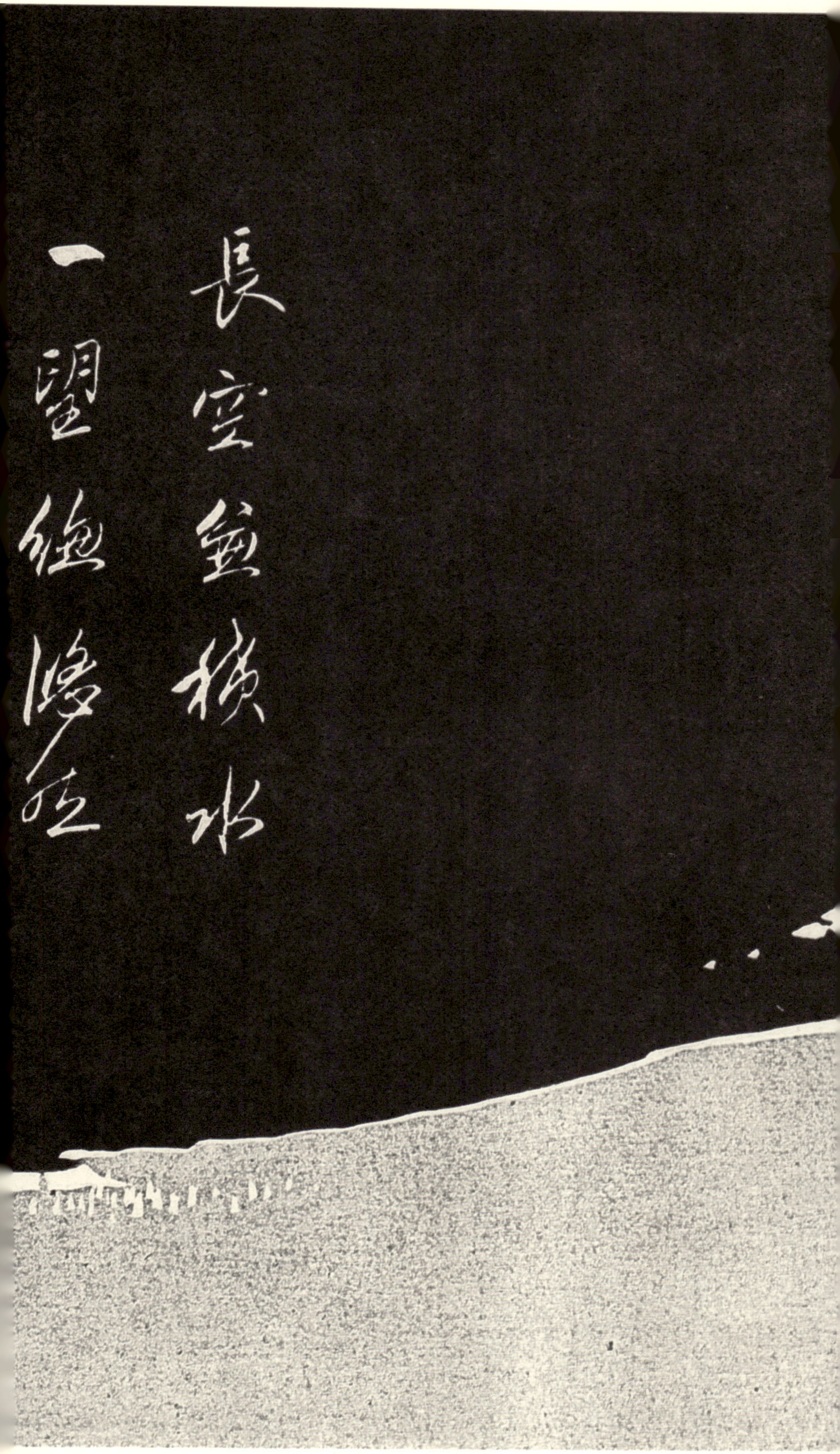

Like a vast ocean, the great heaven
Stretches smoothly like silk as far as the eye sees.

Undulating mountain scenery fading in the distant, pale mist. Houses are scattered here and there with wisps of kitchen smoke.

鳥飼

Birds have flown away where white sails appear.
Trees grow here and there, thatched cottages among them.

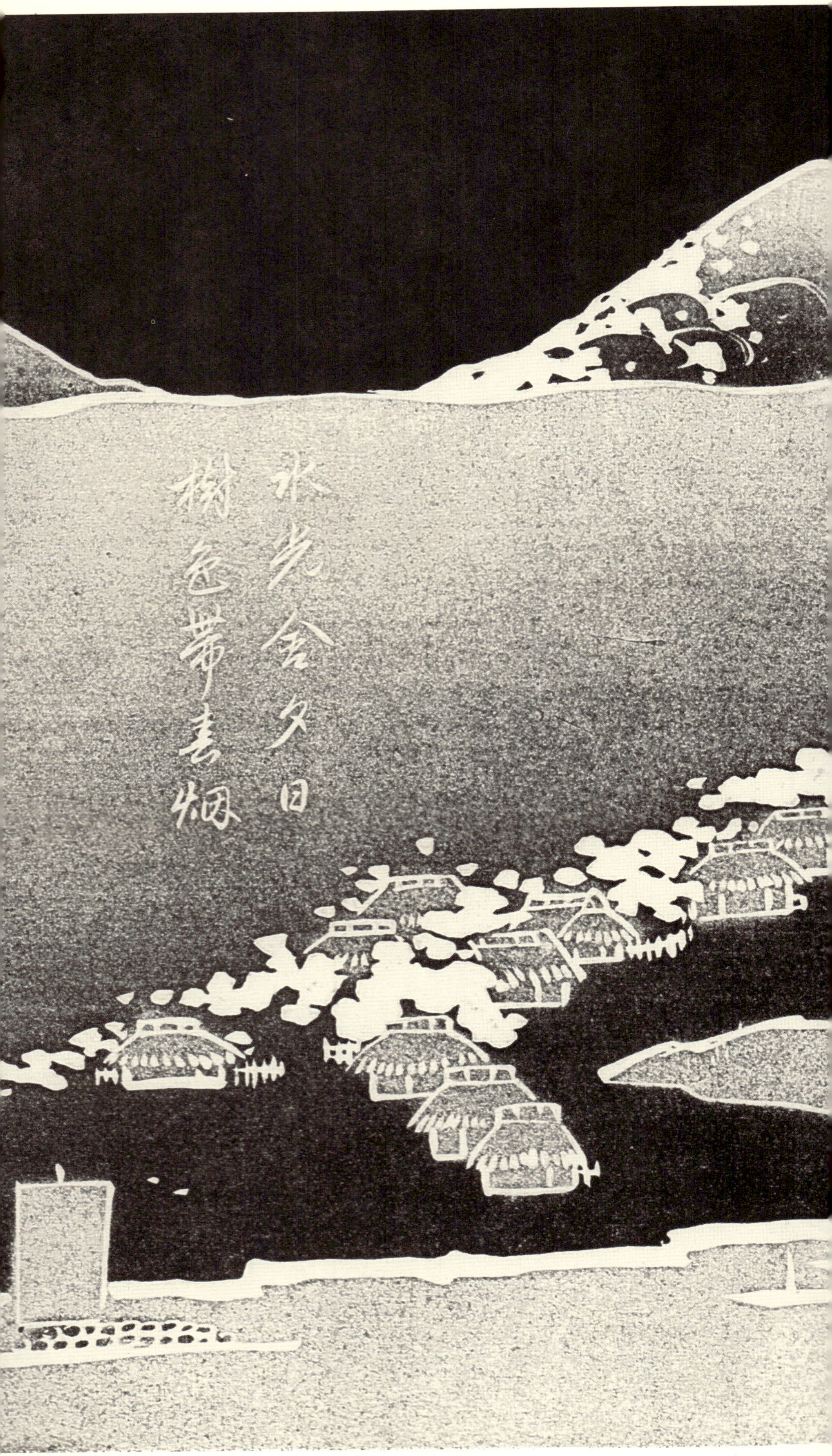

The water reflects the glow of an evening sky.
Trees are veiled in spring mist.

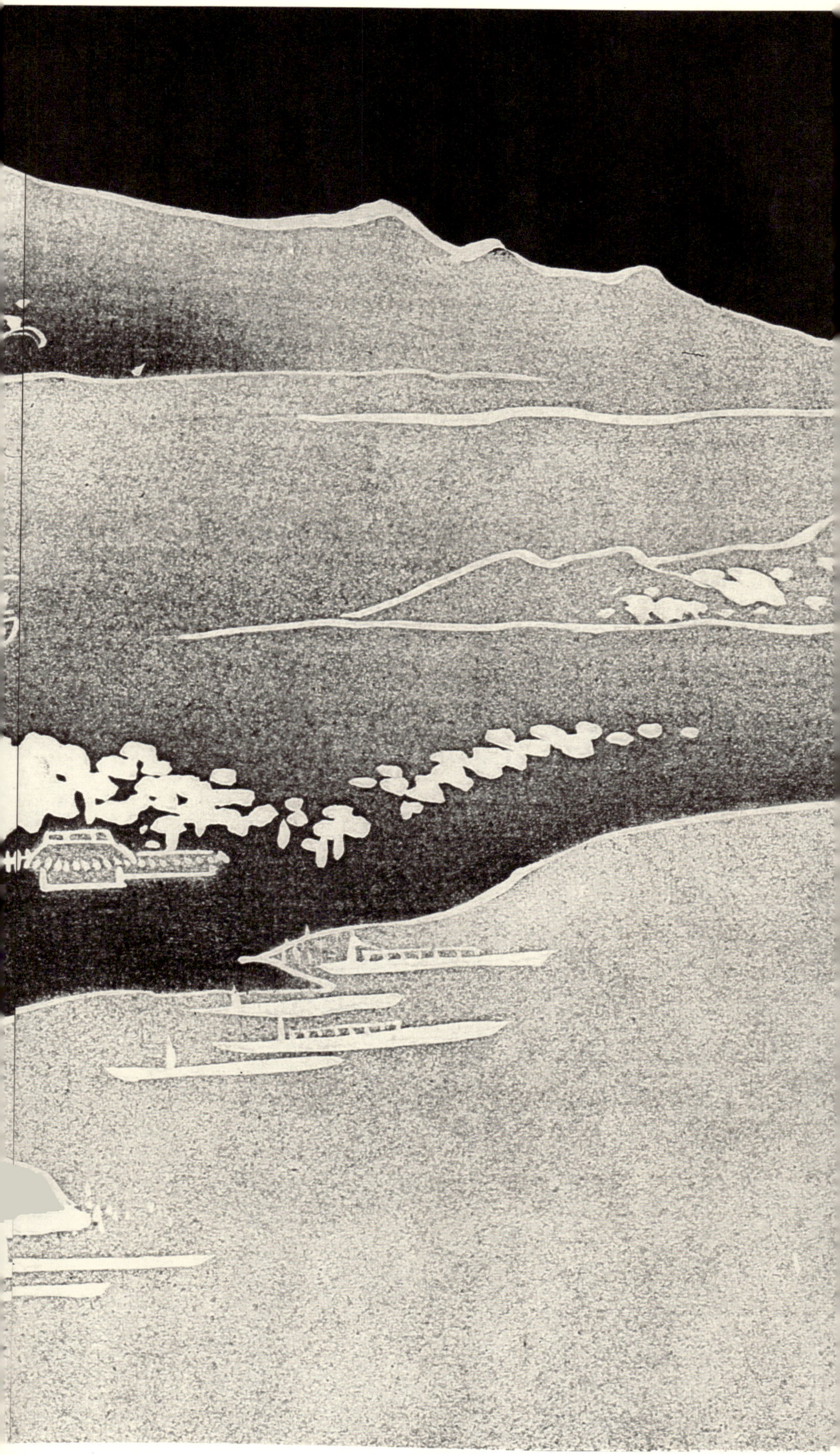

Our waterway leads on and on into the distance.
Far away mountains lie in thick clouds.

大塚

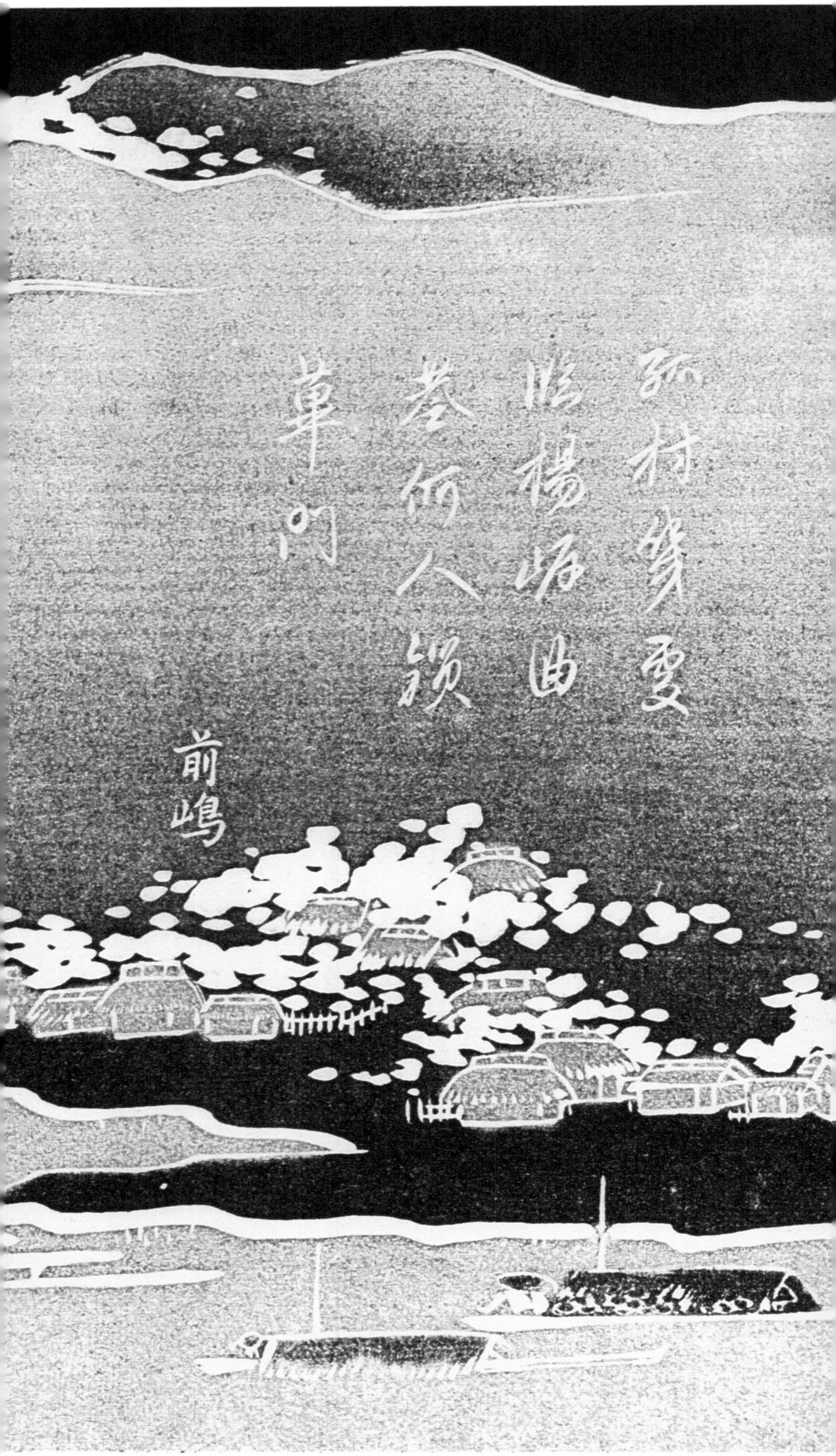

By an isolated village near a bank of willows, where are we now?
Who lives behind the hedge along the narrow crooked lane?

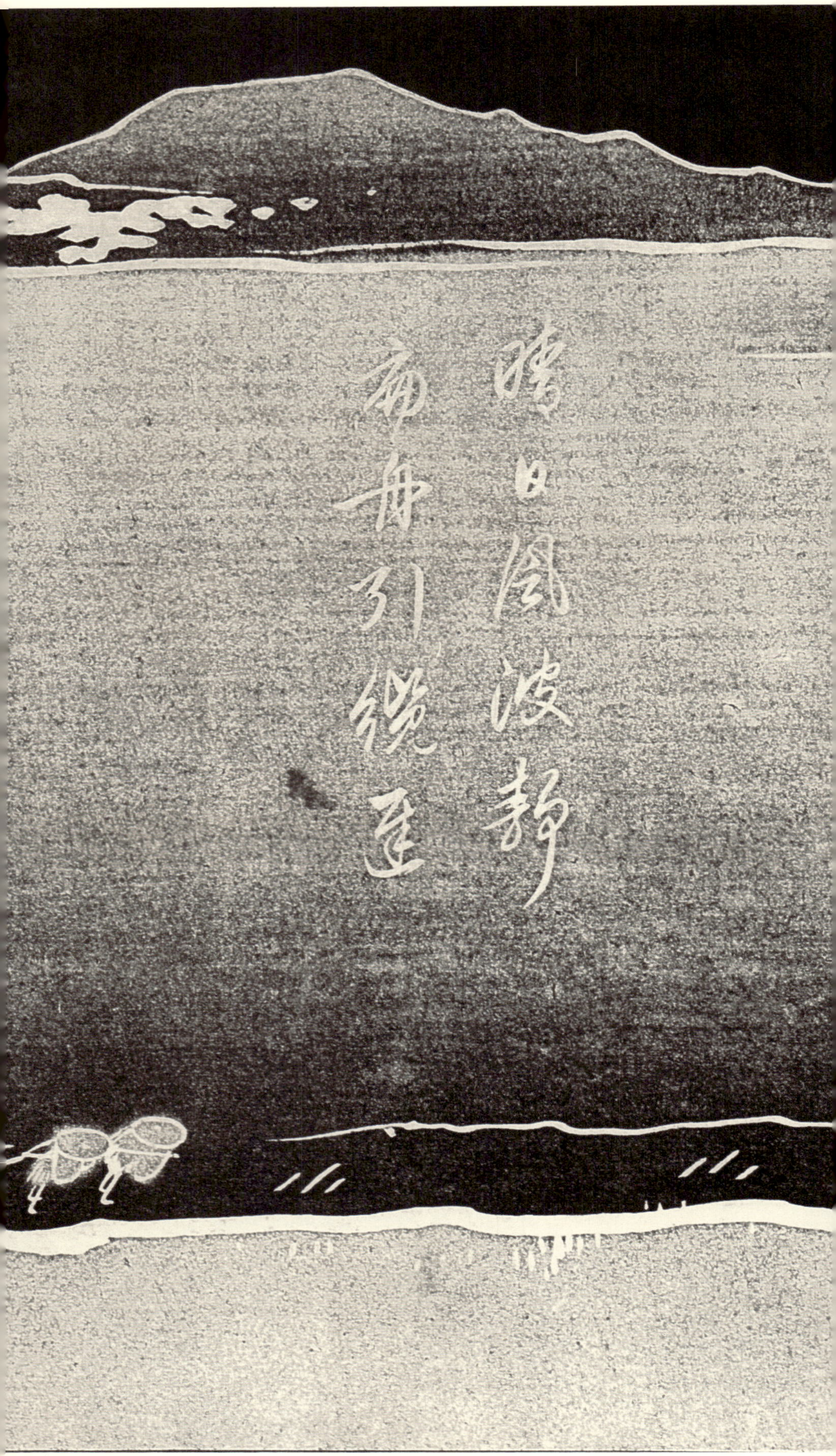

Under the clear sky, wind and waves are still and placid.
A boat moves slowly, towed upstream by lines.

高濱

At an old ferry, no passenger is to be seen.
The boatman is idle, his pole at rest.

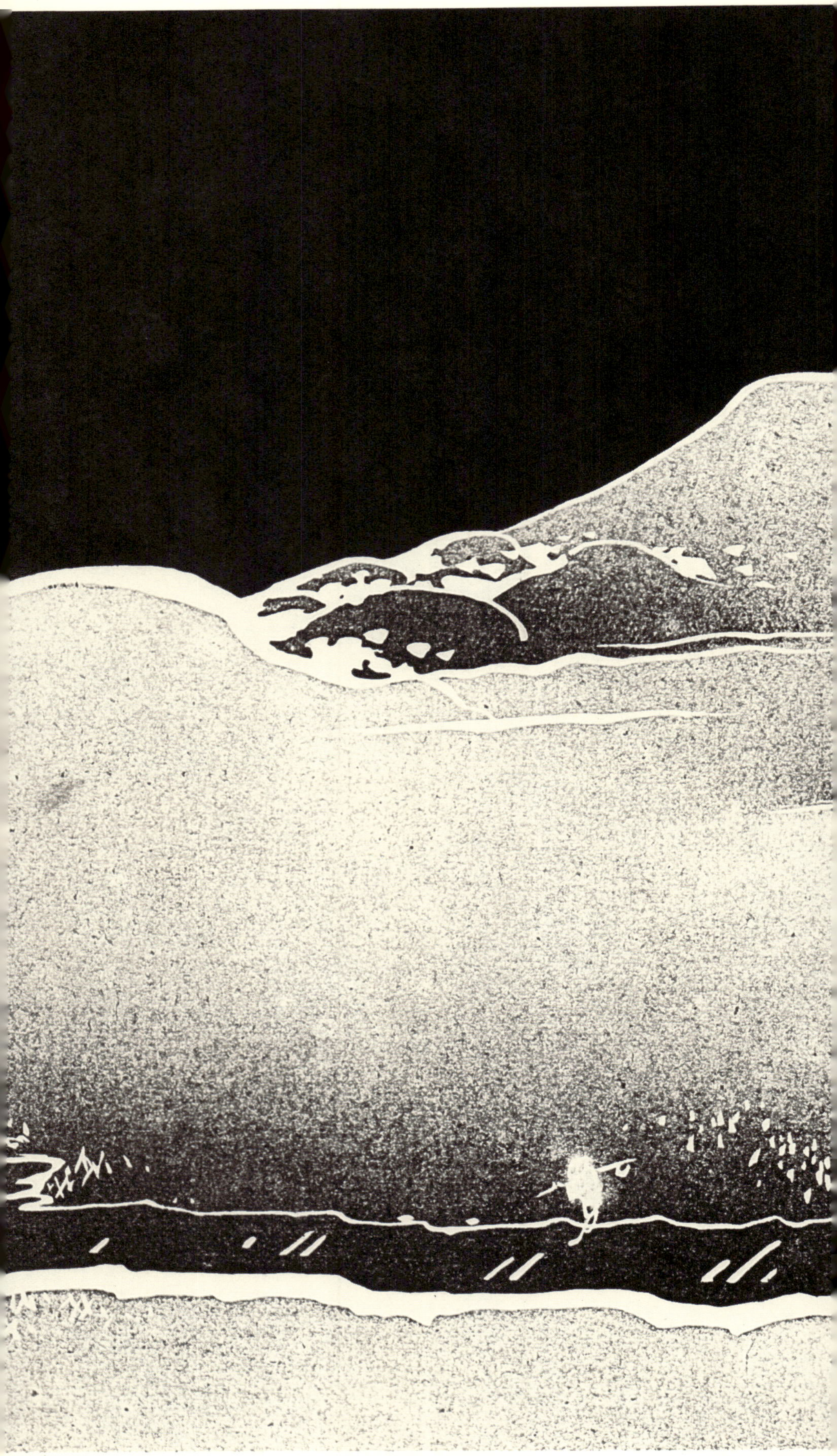

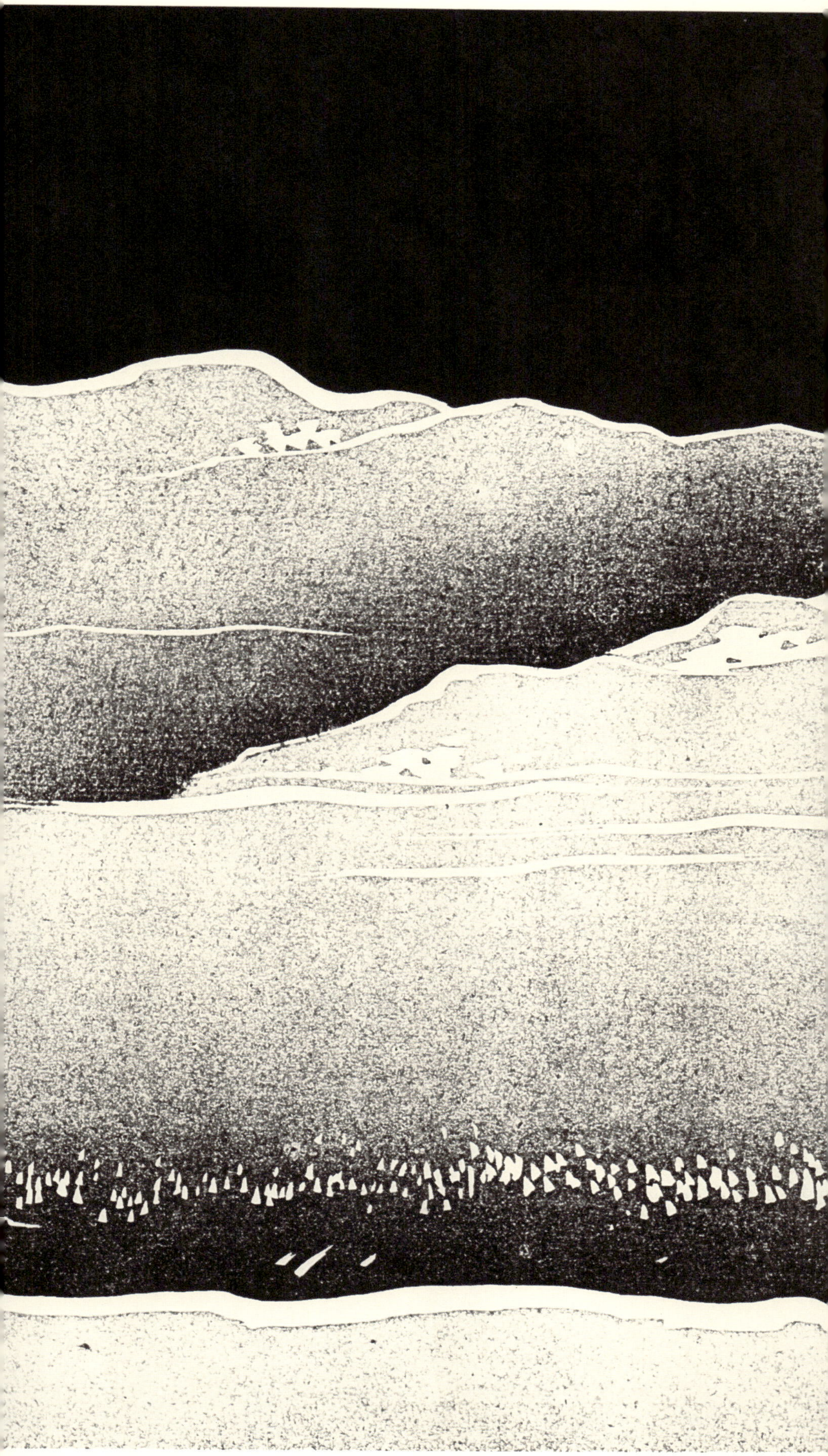

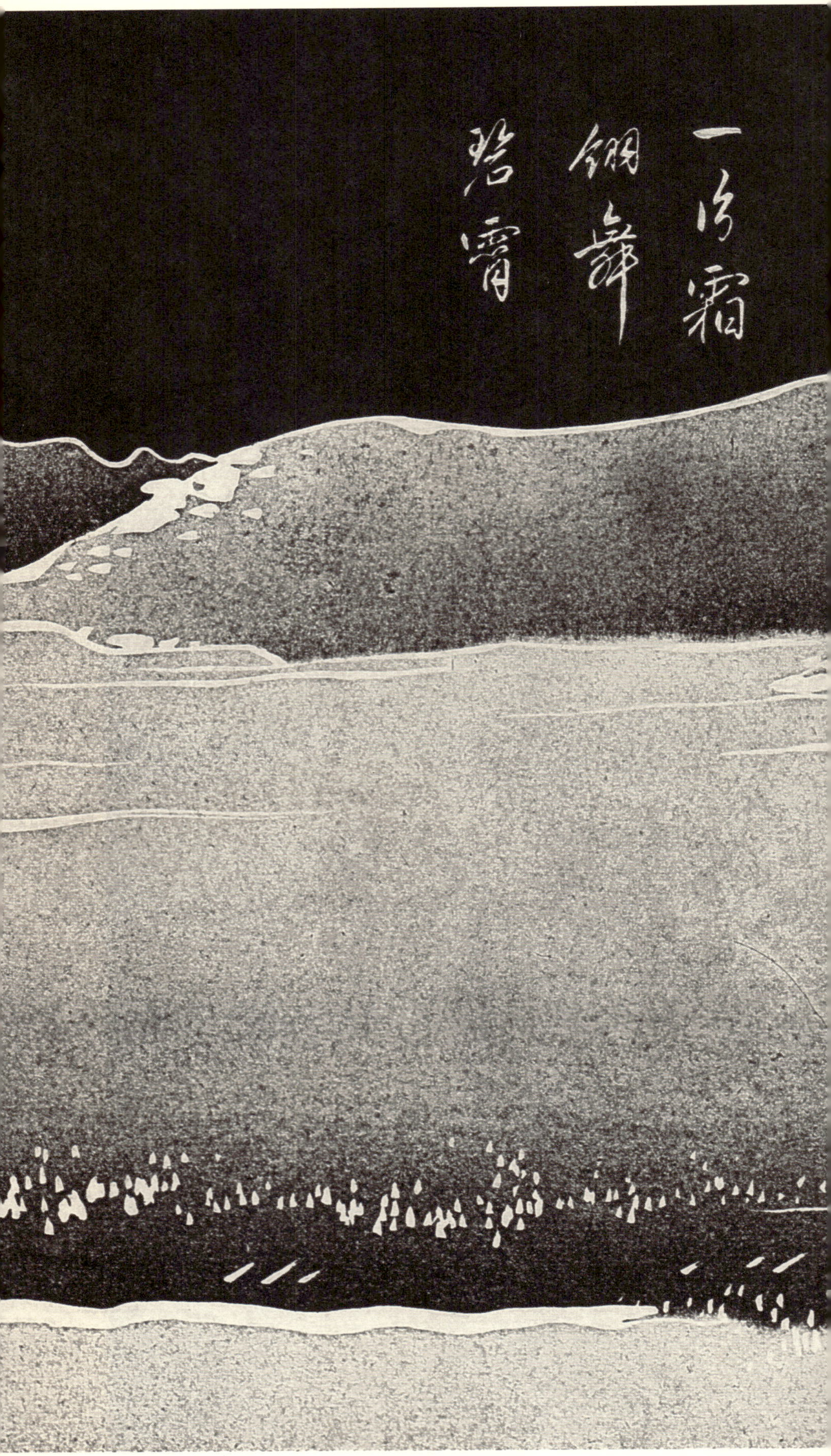

A white crane flies high in the blue sky.

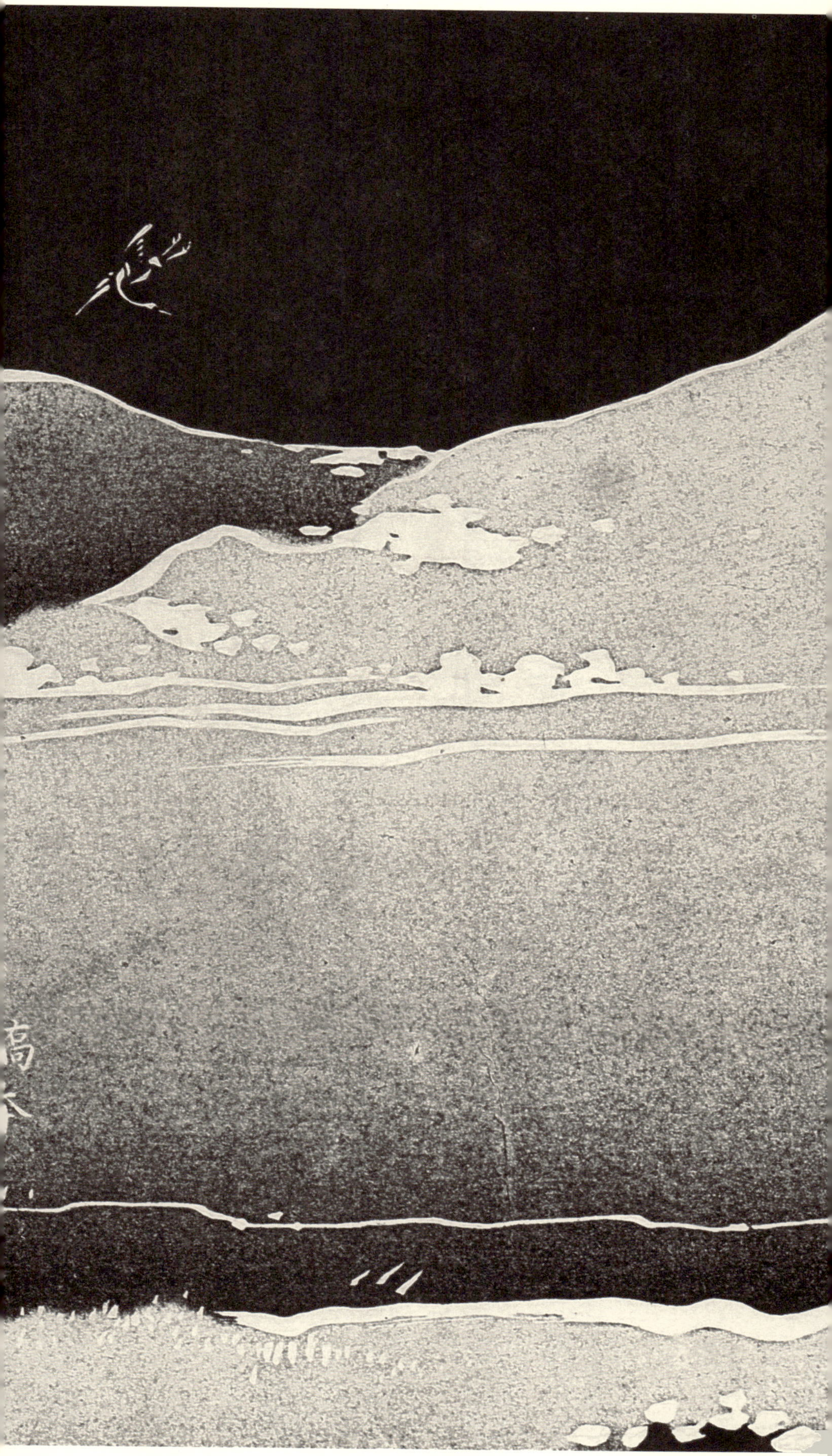

Sacred shrine atop a mountain.
Ancient dwelling of a god, worshiped for millennia.

山崎
八幡

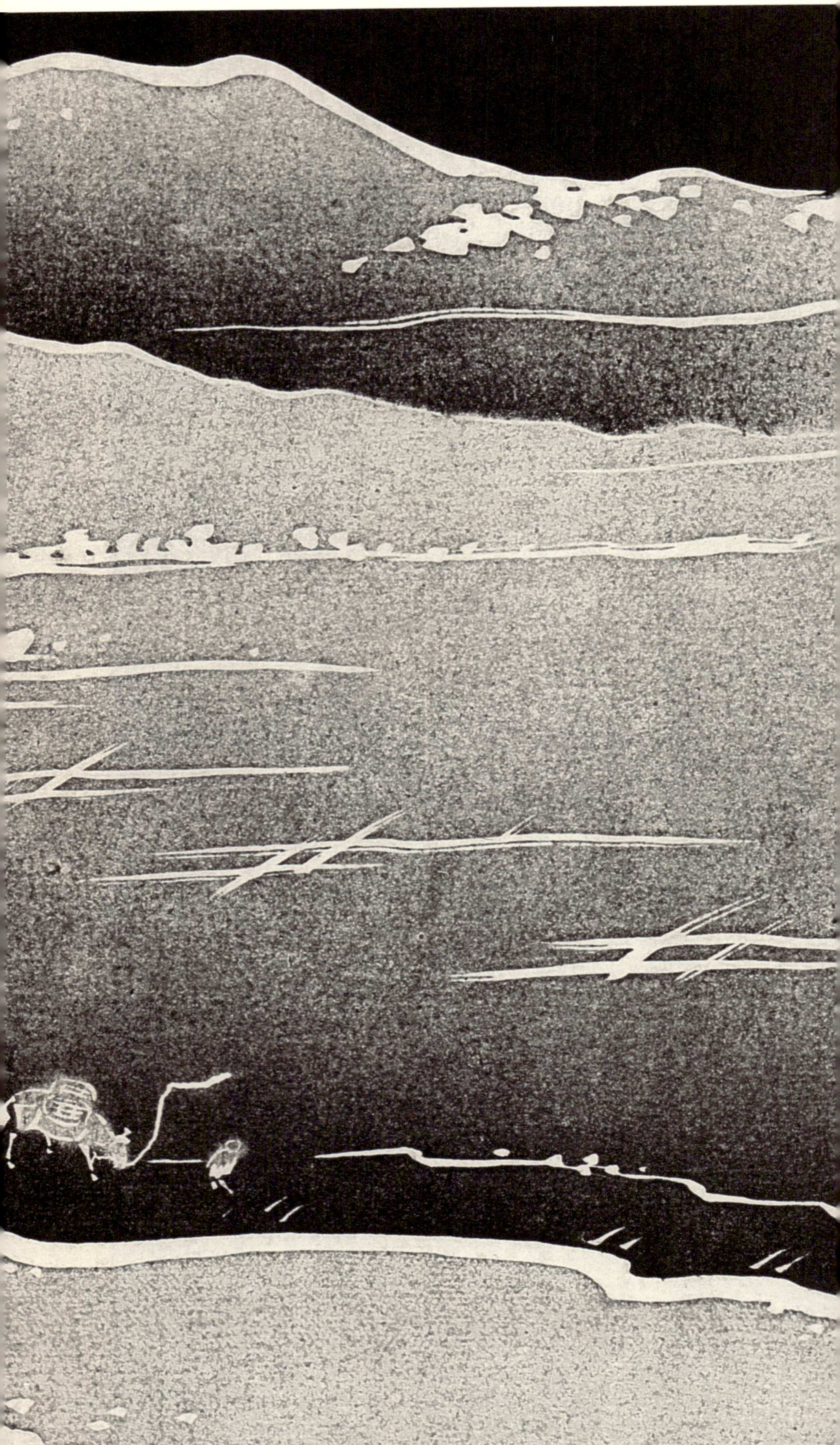

Never tiring of the changing views on our journey,
Our eyes rest briefly on the distant range of steep mountains.

A thousand cottages stand along the Yodogawa.
On the bridge, people are coming and going.

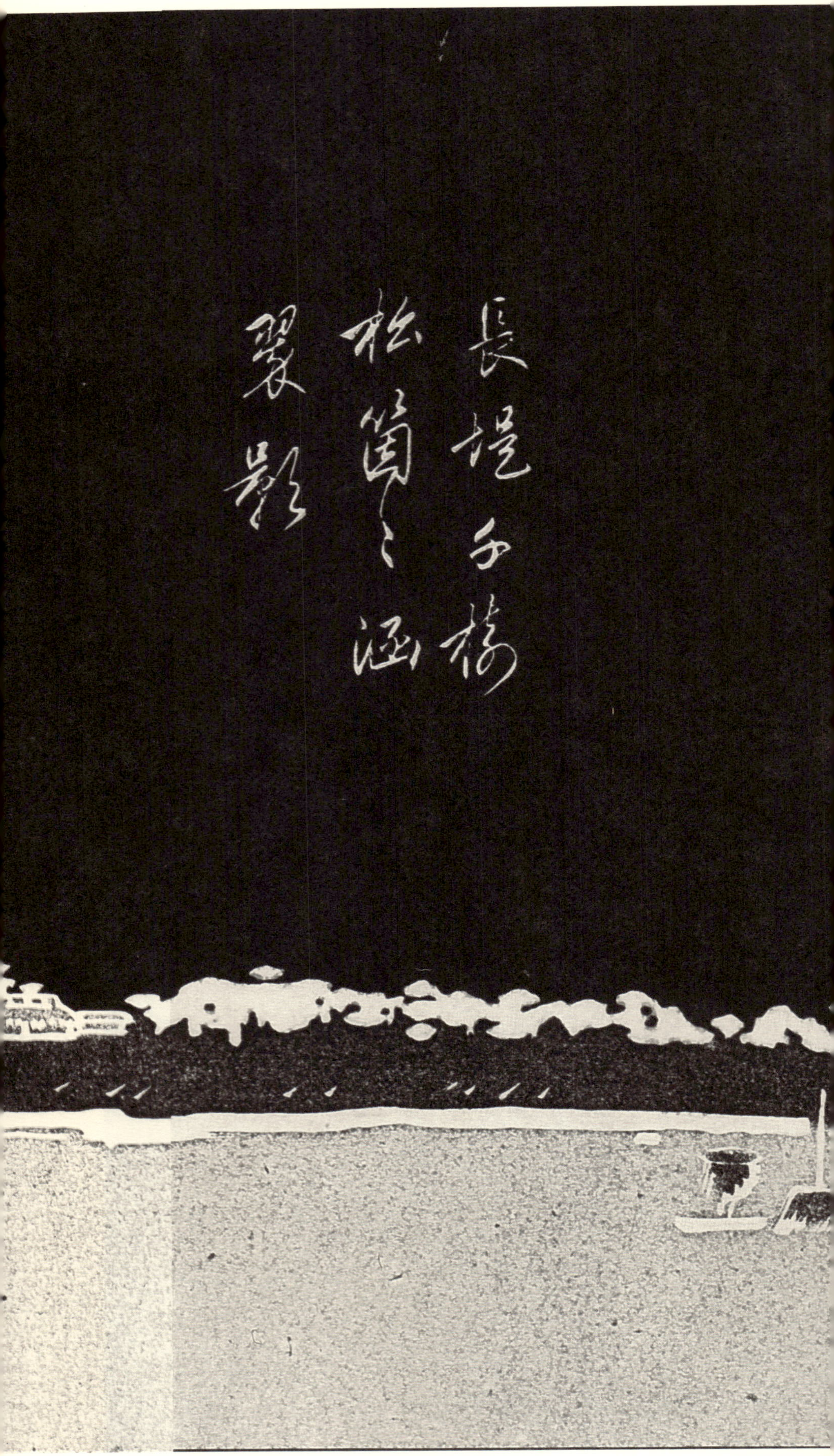

A thousand pine trees stretch along the shore.
Each casts the reflection of its green leaves on the water.

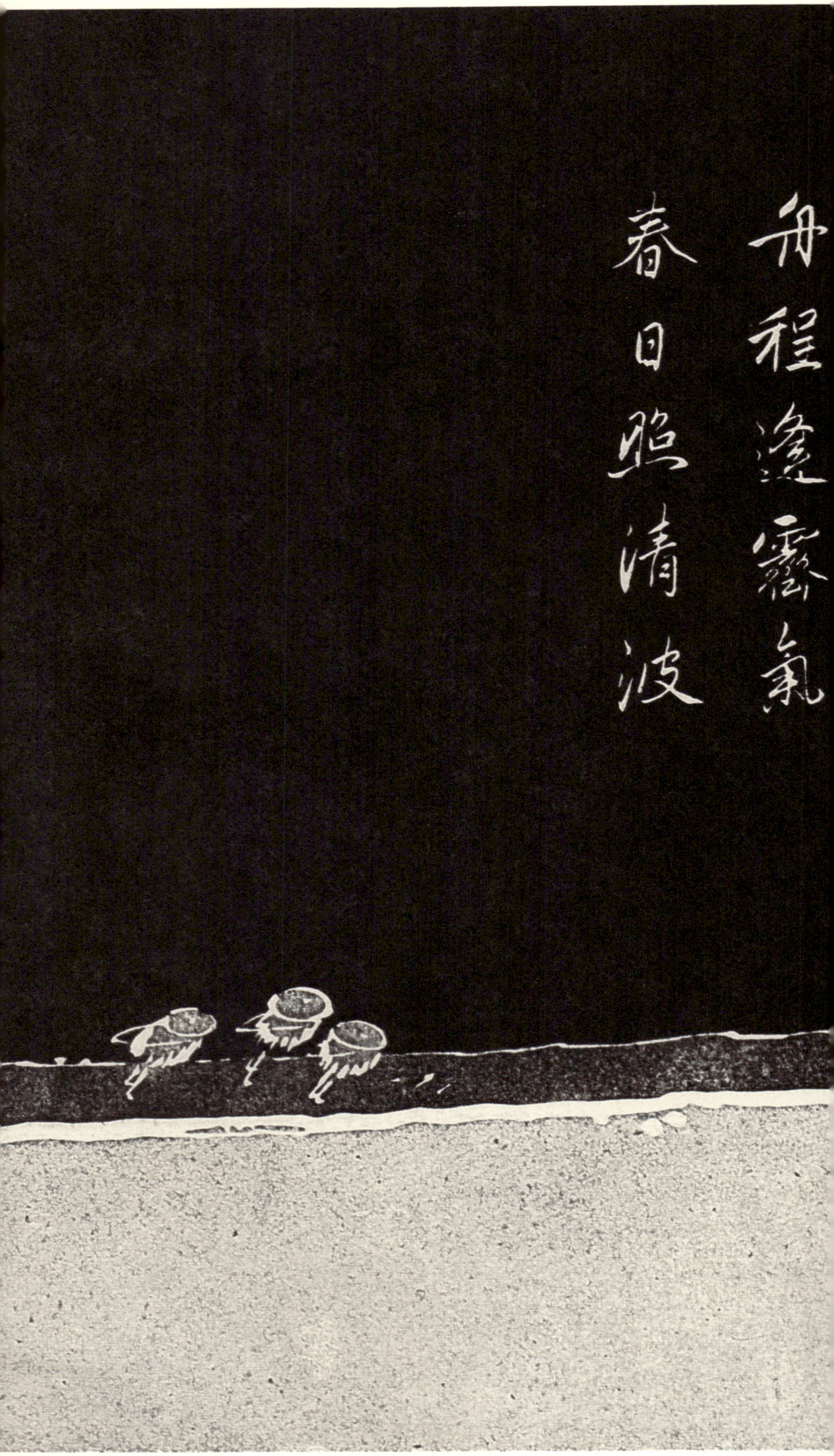

Boating on the river, we are favored by magnificent weather.
The spring sun shines on the transparent water.

伏水口